P9-DDN-697

MORRIS MOLE

DAN YACCARINO

HARPER

An Imprint of HarperCollinsPublishers

There was a mole who lived with his big brothers.

Together they dug.

They ate.

And they slept.

The littlest mole was Morris.

And he was just a bit different from the rest.

One day his biggest brother announced, "We've run out of food!"
"Then we must dig down even farther!" his second biggest brother declared.
The rest of the brothers agreed.

Except for Morris.
"I have an idea!"
But no one heard him.

"Let's go, Brothers!" all the moles shouted. "Dig, dig down! Deep in the ground!"

Morris shouted his idea even louder, but still
no one heard him.
He knew what he had to do.

He was scared,

but

he

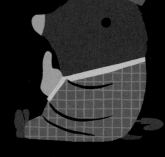

dug

deep

down

and

found

his

courage.

So Morris did something none of his brothers had ever done.

He dug *up*.

And this is what he found.

He had never smelled
anything so sweet,

heard a song so pretty,

met folks
so friendly,

or felt so at peace.

And Morris had never tasted anything so scrumptious.
He was having such a good time he almost forgot why he was there.

So he gathered up all sorts of delicious things to eat, like crunchy creepy crawlies,

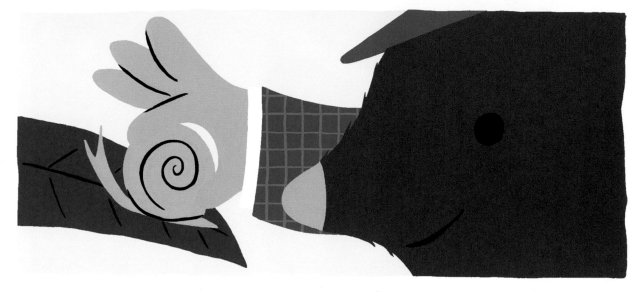

scrumptious snails,

wonderfully
wiggly worms,

tiny tasty fishies,

yummy nuts,
and lovely caterpillars.

And then he picked what he
thought was a particularly big,
beautiful blackberry.

But it wasn't.
It belonged to a very hungry fox. He took one look at
Morris and . . .

was about to swallow him up

in one gulp.

The fox suddenly heard a loud growl.

"Hide me, please!" the fox said.

"Always happy to help," replied Morris.
He began to dig.

And dig and dig and dig.

"Hey, pip-squeak," growled a wolf, "where's that lousy fox?"
"I don't know," Morris said, even though he really did.
So the wolf left.

The fox thanked Morris.

And then he and his friends helped find food for the little mole.

Morris thanked the fox.

Back underground, Morris surprised
his brothers with a feast!

"Great job, Morris," his brothers said.

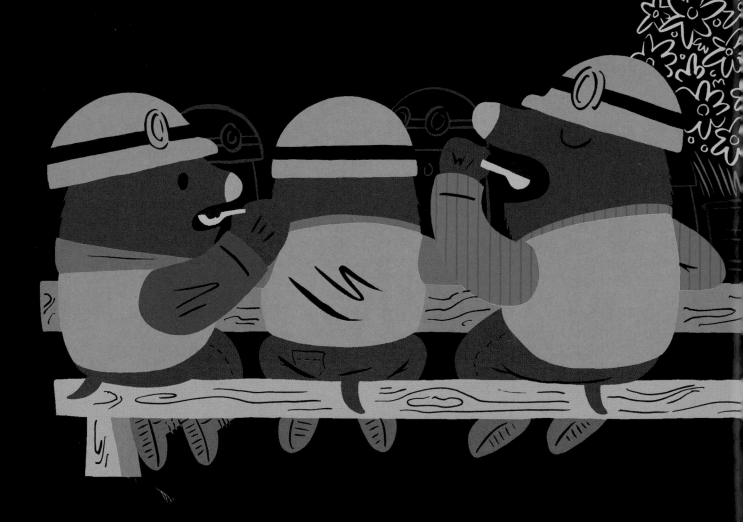

"I may be small," Morris said, "but I can do big things."